Michael Rosen's ABC

Michael Rosen's
ABC

Illustrated by Bee Willey

Published in the United States in 1996 by

The Millbrook Press, Inc.
2 Old New Milford Road
Brookfield, Connecticut 06804

First published in Great Britain in 1995 by

Macdonald Young Books
Campus 400
Maylands Avenue
Hemel Hempstead HP2 7EZ

Edited by Wendy Knowles
Designed by David Fordham

Library of Congress Cataloging-in-Publication Data

Rosen, Michael, 1946–
    Michael Rosen's ABC / illustrated by Bee Willey.
        p.   cm.
    Summary: Combines nonsense poems and fanciful illustrations with
objects representing each letter of the alphabet.
    ISBN 1–56294–138–0 (lib. bdg.)   0–7613–0127–5 (tr.)
    1. Children's poetry, English.   2. English language—Alphabet—
Juvenile literature.   3. Alphabet rhymes.   [1. Nonsense verses.
2. English poetry.   3. Alphabet.   4. Picture puzzles.]   I. Willey,
Bee, ill.   II. Title.
PR6068.068M53   1996
821′.914[E]—dc20
                                                          96–12468
                                                          CIP
                                                          AC

Printed by Wing King Tong, Hong Kong

Come into a magic wood
where you might meet anything
from the man in the moon
          to an octopus,
Goldilocks or birds that sing

And you know that alphabets
          go A to Z
which means you'll have to look
for ants and zebras hiding
on every page of this book

If you turn to the pages
          at the back
you can check out what's on the list
so when you spot who's in the picture
you'll see if there's any you've missed

A a

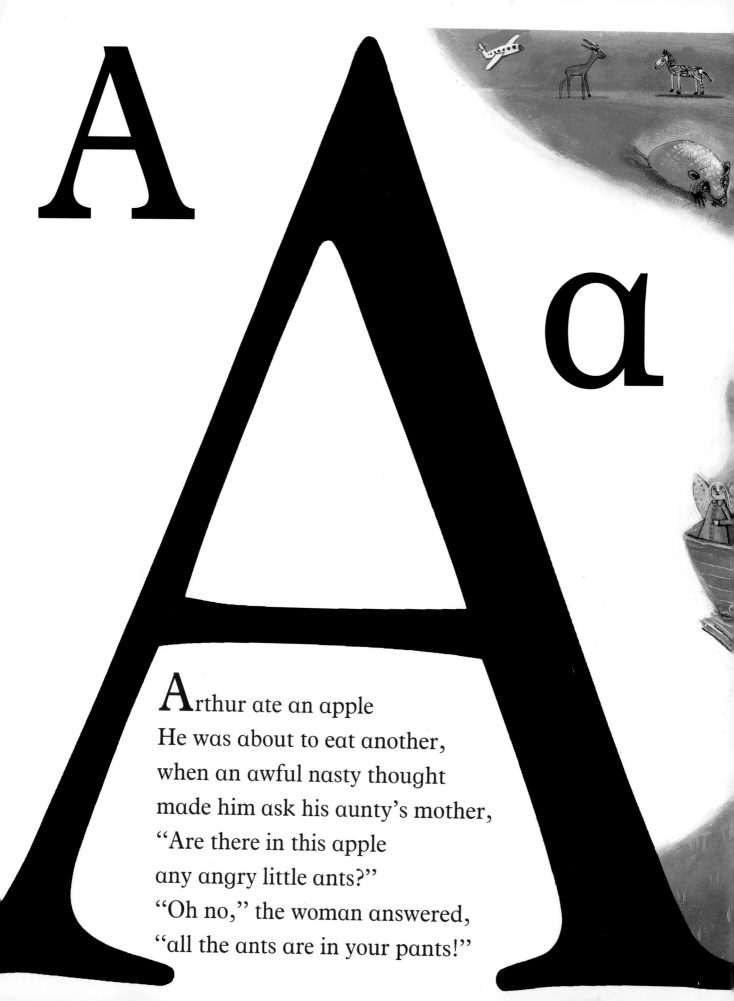

Arthur ate an apple
He was about to eat another,
when an awful nasty thought
made him ask his aunty's mother,
"Are there in this apple
any angry little ants?"
"Oh no," the woman answered,
"all the ants are in your pants!"

"Bumble bees buzz,"
bellowed busy Biddy,
banging out the beat:
Bal-am bamba diddy.

"Belly buttons boring,"
blurted out Brenda,
bouncing on the bed:
Boo-wa ba-lenda.

"Bottom bunk's best,"
burbled bouncy Beulah,
blowing out bubbles:
Be-bop ba-lula.

Charlie Chaplin chewed a cake.
Could the cake that Charlie chewed
be the cake that Charlie chose?

If the crows that Charlie caught
were the crows that chose the cake
then the cake was chewed by crows.

But if the crows that chose the cake
chewed the cake that Charlie chose,
could the crows that chewed the cake
be the crows that Charlie chose?

C

D

Dolly dipped dollies in the rain.

Dennis dropped his dinner down the drain.

Donna danced with donkeys in the park.

Drew dreamt of dragons in the dark.

Doris dressed her dog in a shirt.

Dudley dragged his dad through the dirt.

d

Ee

"Each of these elephants has elastic legs.
Every eagle you see lays plastic eggs.
All of the eels have electric eyes
That elm tree is really an elk in disguise.
Everything else that you see is enchanted.
Even the trees were magically planted."
Electric? Wow!
That eagle! The beak!
Elastic? Incredible!
Those eels! Eeeek!

F f

Frightful Friday,
fairly foggy,
forest freezing—
frozen Froggie.

Froggie feels
feet freeze;
fancies food—
follows fleas.

Fleas frightened.
Fleas flee.
Fleas fast—
fleas free.

Freezing Friday,
fairly foggy,
forest freezing—
fed up Froggie.

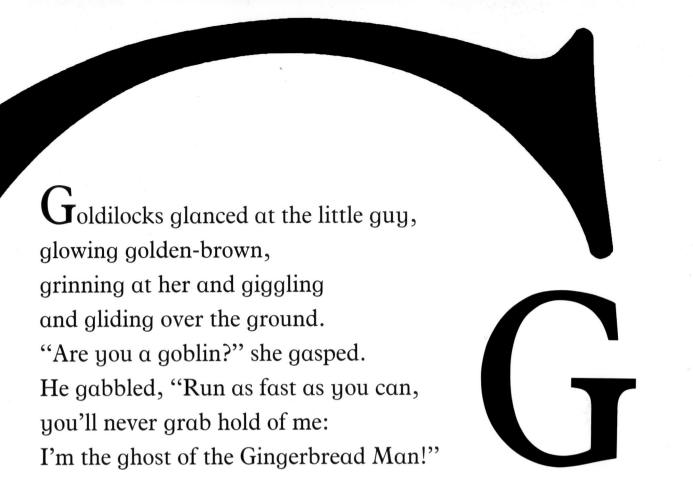

Goldilocks glanced at the little guy,
glowing golden-brown,
grinning at her and giggling
and gliding over the ground.
"Are you a goblin?" she gasped.
He gabbled, "Run as fast as you can,
you'll never grab hold of me:
I'm the ghost of the Gingerbread Man!"

H

Humpty Dumpty had a headache
it hurt his head like mad,
he heard a hat would help
and hurried to his dad.

But Humpty's dad has no hair
and hates it with his hat off;
having no hat upon his head,
makes him have a cough.

So Humpty has a headache
and he doesn't have a hat.
His dad has got no hair
and that, my friends, is that.

h

Ivan the Terrible is ill.
Ivan's insides are twitching.
The Doctor inspects Ivan
and sees that his skin is itching.

The Doctor says, "Poison Ivy!"
and covers Ivan in ice.
Ivan the Terrible yells, "Idiot!"
then something not very nice.

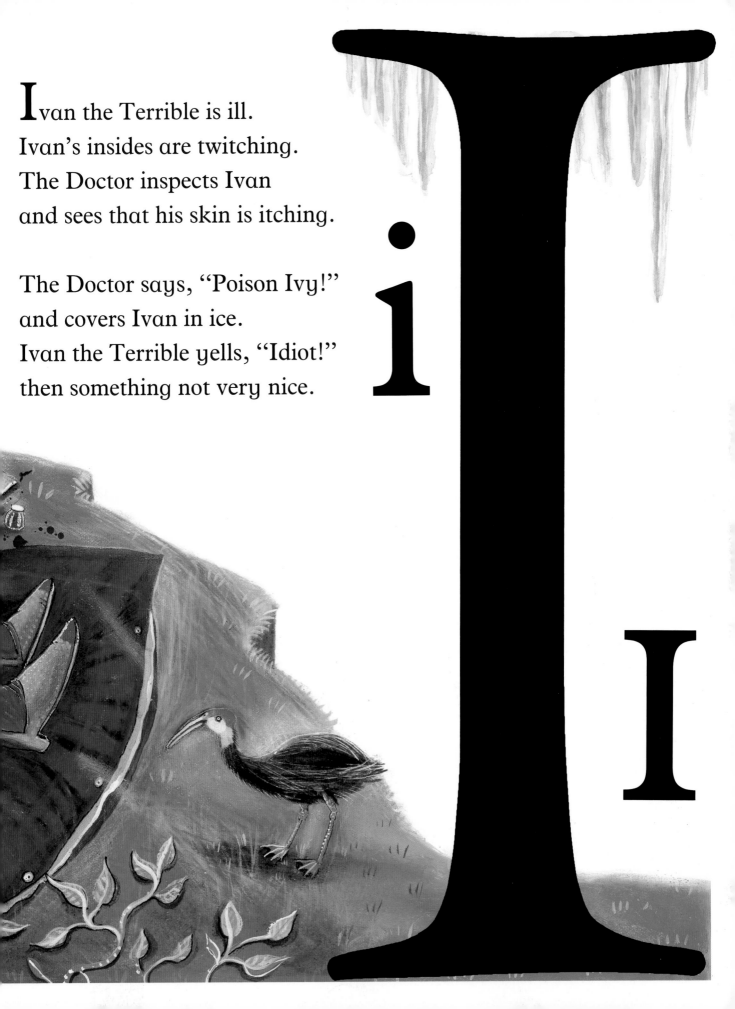

J j

Jack and Jill went up the hill
Juggling a jug of jelly.
A passing bug jumped in the jug
which made the jelly smelly.

Jack's hands stopped, the jug just dropped.
He sat and jibbered, "It broke!"
This now means, he tore his jeans,
which Jack said wasn't a joke.

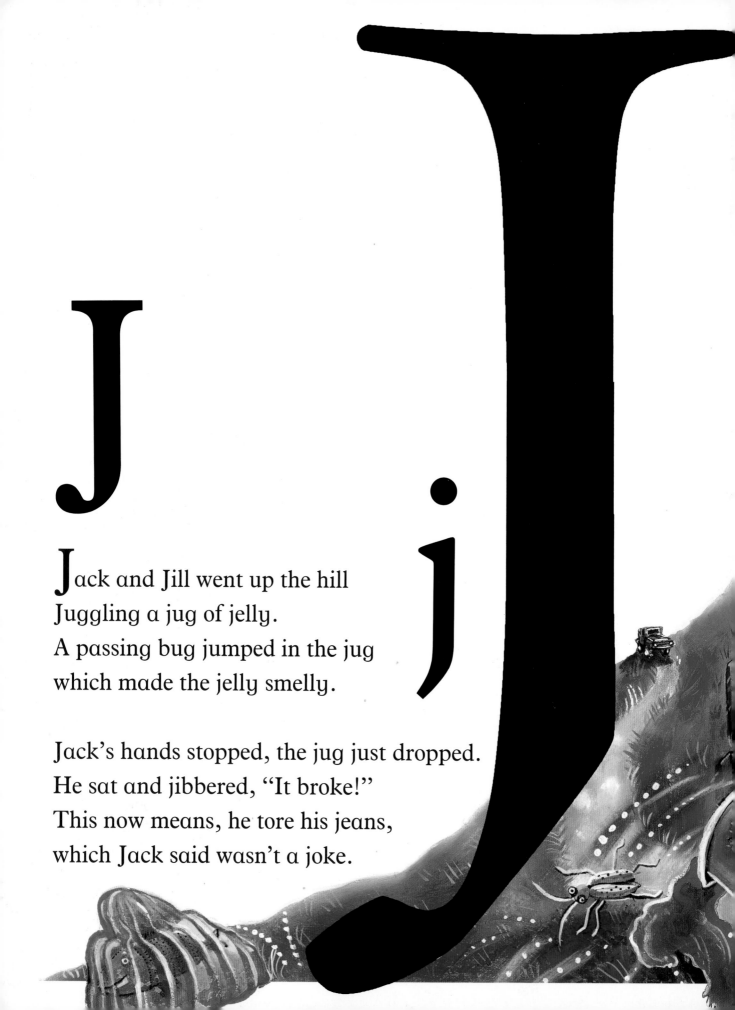

K k

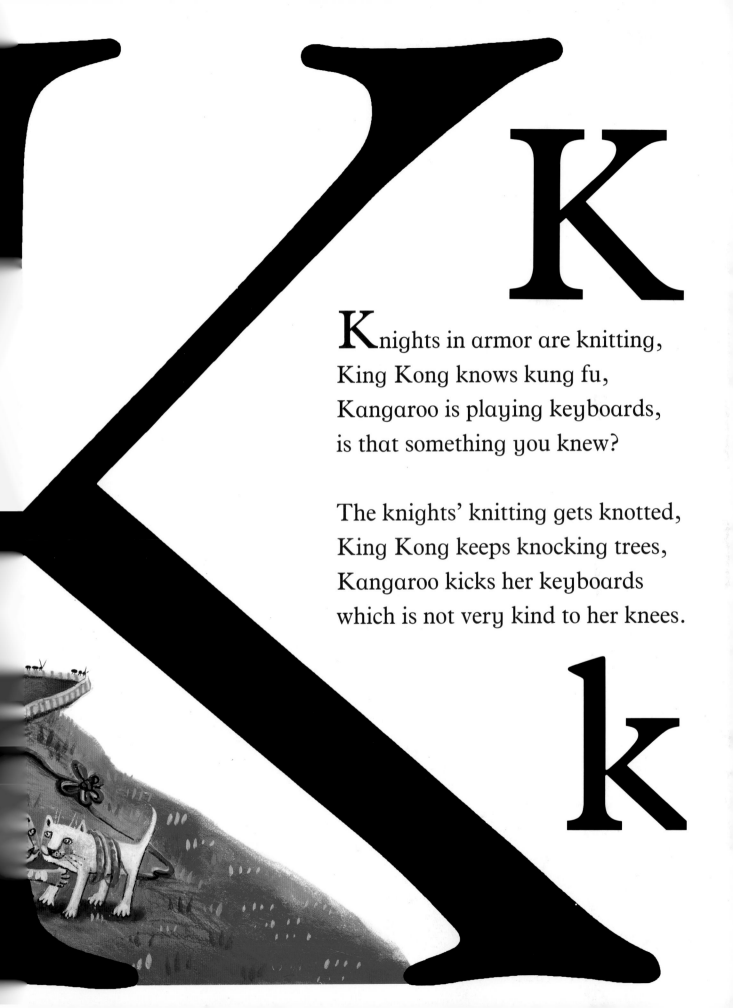

Knights in armor are knitting,
King Kong knows kung fu,
Kangaroo is playing keyboards,
is that something you knew?

The knights' knitting gets knotted,
King Kong keeps knocking trees,
Kangaroo kicks her keyboards
which is not very kind to her knees.

Little Red Riding Hood lost her lunch
and the letter for the Lady of the Lake.
That lion with a limp looks just like a dog
Is he lying when he says he loves cake?

The lunch and the letter she left by the log
That odd-looking lion is laughing a lot
till Little Red Riding Hood lifts his lips
and learns exactly what's what.

So the wolf leapt up and down the lane:
it wasn't his lucky day.
Little Red Riding Hood was a little late
And the lesson is: lions aren't gray.

Ll

Mother Goose met Little Miss Muffet
in the middle of the night.
They made magic music
until morning light.

The Monkey said, "Meow."
The Mole said, "Moo."
The Magpie's got the measles
and the Monster got you.

Singing:
"May mumble duddle
The Mole's in a muddle
The Mouse jumped over the moon.
The little Moth laughed
to see such a mess
and the milk ran away with the spoon."

N
n

N orman says Nelly is noisy
and natters all night with the nurse.
But Nelly says Norman is nosy
which Nelly says is much worse.

Nosy or noisy, which is worse?
Nobody here can choose.
Nothing else has happened.
That's the end of the news.

Oliver was an orphan
once upon a time.
Oh dear! Oh dear! Oh dear!
Our hero turned to crime.

You ought not to worry.
It's often this way.
It was only in a book,
so it turned out OK.

Pp

"Pardon me," said the pigeon,
"I was playing with a pie."
The peacock wasn't pleased
as a piece plopped in his eye.

The penguin picked it out
but then she went and dropped it.
Along came the pelican
and in his mouth he popped it.

Q

"Quack quack," said the duck.
"Quick quick," said the quail.
"Be quiet," said the Queen.
"Don't quarrel," said the snail.

"Aren't I first in the queue?"
said the Queen to the quail.
"What a stupid question!"
said the duck to the snail.

"Quite right!" said the quads.
"Who asked you?" said the quail.
"Aren't I in charge?" said the Queen.
"Is this a quiz?" said the snail.

q

Rudolph the Red-Nosed Reindeer
relaxed after a really rough ride.
A river rippled round some rocks
and he stared at the road, red-eyed.

Robin Hood and Robin Redbreast,
a raven and some other birds
were running down the road toward him
waving and roaring rude words.

Both Rudolph and I
often wonder why.

Snow White saw a squirrel
and the squirrel saw a sheep.
The sheep saw a snake
who seemed to be asleep.

But Sheep stood on Snake
and Snake started to hiss.
Squirrel started squeaking
and Snow White said this:

"If Sheep said sorry
and Squirrel stopped squeaking,
Snake would go back to sleep
and I'd stop speaking."

T om Thumb, Tom Thumb
take care! take care!
A terrific tarantula
is just over there.

No need to tell Tom.
Tom Thumb knows.
Tarantula's his friend
and Tom tickles his toes.

Uu

Unicorns used to stand under trees.
Unicorns used to understand trees.
Unicorns couldn't usually climb right up trees.
Unicorns couldn't usually climb upright trees.
Unicorns said: "Unfair! There are no stairs up trees."
Unicorns said: "Unfair! There are no upstairs trees."

Did unicorns really understand trees?

V v

Vultures don't eat vegetables
vultures don't eat greens
vultures don't eat carrots
vultures don't eat beans.

Vultures eat what's dead
as everybody knows.
Volcanoes are often very dead.
Do vultures eat volcanoes?

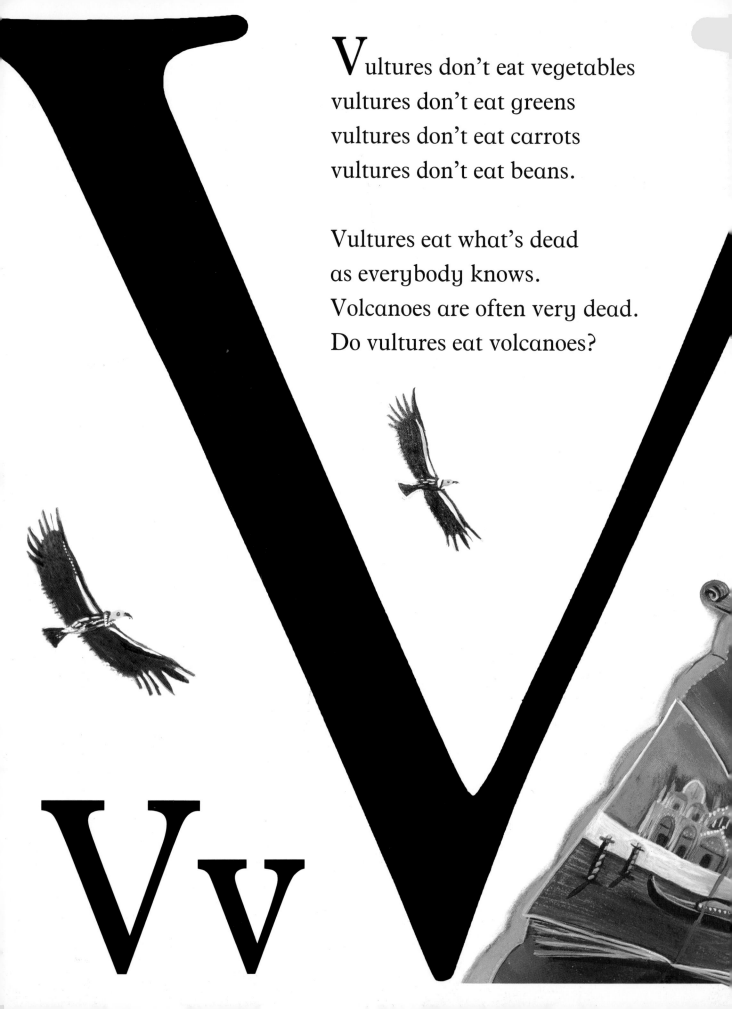

W ee Willie Winkie whispered
          why? why? why?
Where is the wind?
And who am I?

Wee Willie Winkie whispered
          when? when? when?
Which one is winter?
And what am I then?

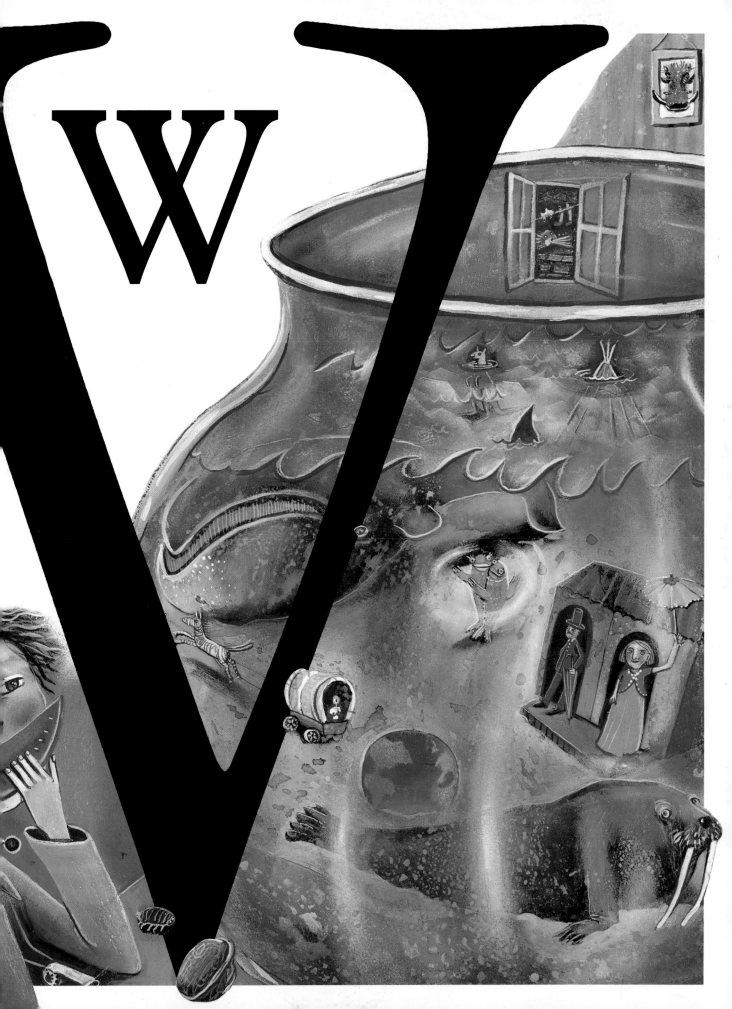

X marks the spot on the X-ray.
You can hear old hippo moan.

She really shouldn't have swallowed
her brand new xylophone.

Y y

Yankee Doodle came to town
riding on a yak.
He stuck a yo-yo in his cap
and called it yackety-yack.

Yankee Doodle lost his cap
(you know the kind of fellow).
He yelled like mad till he went blue
but the yo-yo is plain yellow.

Z

Zoom! goes the zebra.
He's escaped from the zoo.
Forty keepers are after him
what should he do?

He zigzags through the forest.
He hopes the keepers will trip.
He dreams he could take off his coat
by pulling down a zip.

Word lists

A

abacus
ace
acorn
acrobat
airplane
albatross
alligator
amethyst
anaconda
anchor
angel
animals (*in ark*)
ankle
antelope
ants
ape
apple
apricot
armadillo
armchair
armor
arrow
Arthur
artichoke
atlas (*Africa*)
avocado

B

baby (*badger*)
badger
bag
ball
ballerina
ballet shoe
balloons
bananas
bangers (*sausages*)
banjo
bark
basket
bat
bath
beads
beans
bears (*the Three Bears*)
bed
bedsprings
bees
bell
beret
berries
Beulah
Biddy
bird
biscuits
blackberries
blackbird
blanket
blooms
blow
blue
boat
bones
bonfire (*blazing*)
book

boots
bottle
bow
bowls
boy (*Little Boy Blue*)
bracelet
braid
branch
bread and butter
breeches
Brenda
bridge
brontosaurus
bubble
bucket
buds
burst (*balloon*)
bush
butterfly
button

C

cabbage
cage
cake
camel
camera
candles
carpet
carrots
cart

cartwheel
castle
cat
catapult
caterpillars
chair
Charlie Chaplin
checkerboard
checkered
cheesecake
chef
cherries
chess
chicken
chicks
chimes
chopped (*nuts in cake*)
circles
claws
clock
cloth
cloud
coat
coconut
cravat
cream
crimson
crocus
crown
crows
cucumbers
cup
curly hair

D

dad
daffodils
dagger
daisy
dance
dart
dart board
date
dates
dawn
deck chair
denim
Dennis
dew (*on grass*)
diamond
diary
dice
dinner
dinosaur
dipping
dirt
dish
doctor's bag
dogs (*dachshund
    and dalmatian*)
doll
Dolly
dolphin
domino
donkey
Donna
Doris
dots
doughnuts
dove
dozen
Dracula
dragging

dragon
drain
drawing
dream
dress (*dirndl*)
Drew
drill
drops of rain
    (*dripping*)
duck
duckling
Dudley

E

eagles
ears
earthworms
ear trumpet
Easter eggs
eclairs
eclipse
eggcup
eggs
Egypt
eight
elastic
electric eels
electric lights
elephants
eleven o'clock
elk
elm
emu
entrance

explorer
explosion
eyes

F

face
falcon
family (*of fish*)
farm
fence
ferns
ferret
field
fig
fingers
fir cones
fir tree
fish
fish pond
flag
flamingo
fleas (*five*)
float
flock (*of sheep*)
flowers
flute
flying
foal
fog
foliage
football
footprints

forest
fork
fountain
four (*frogs*)
fox
foxgloves
frogs
Frost (*Jack Frost
    playing the flute*)
frozen
fruit
fur

G

galleon
garden
gardener
gardenia
garland
gate
gazelle
geese
geraniums
giant
gingerbread house
gingerbread man
gingham
giraffe
girl
glass
glasses
glowworms
goat

goblin
gold
goldfish
goldfish bowl
Goldilocks
golf ball
gooseberry pie
grapefruit
grass
gravel
gray squirrel
green
greyhound
grin
ground
guitar
gum boots

H

hair
half
hamburger
hammock
hamper
hamster
handbag
handkerchief
handle
hands
happy (*hippos*)
hare
harlequin (*in hammock*)
harp

harvest
hats
hawk
hay
hazelnuts
head
hearts
hedge
helicopter
hens
hidden (*chick*)
hills
hippopotamus
hive
holding
hole
holly
honey
honeysuckle
horn
horse
house
Humpty Dumpty
hundred
hutch

I

ibis
ice
iceberg
ice cream
icicles
igloo
iguana

immobile (*Ivan*)
incognito (*doctor*)
indigo
ink
inkblots
inkwell
insects
inside
instrument
iris
iron
island (*in shape of India*)
Ivan
ivy (*poison ivy*)

J

Jack
jackdaw (*bird*)
jack-in-the-box
jaguar
jam
jars
jeans
jeep
jellied fish
jelly
jellybean
jester
jigsaw
Jill
jockey
jodhpurs
joust

Judy (*as in "Punch and Judy"*)
jug
juggling
jumper
jungle

K

kaleidoscope
kangaroo
kayak
ketchup
kettle
keyboard
keyhole
keys
kicking
kid
kilt
kimono
king
kingfisher
King Kong
kiosk
kiss
kittens
kiwi
kiwi fruit
knapsack
knave
kneeling
knees
knickerbocker glory (*ice cream*)

knights
knitting
knocked down tree
knot
koala
kung fu

L

lace
laces
ladle
ladybirds (*in love*)
lake
lambs
lamp
lane
laurel wreath
leaves
leeks
lemons
letter
lids
light
lilacs
lily
lime
limp
lion
lips
lizard
lobster
locusts
logs
long hair

looking glass
lunch
lyre

M

magic
magic carpet
magic wand
magpie
mandolin
man in the moon
map
maraca
marbles
Mars (*planet*)
mask
measles
meringues
mermaid
milk
Miss Muffet
mole
monkey
monster hands
moon
moon craters
mop
Mother Goose
moths
mountains
mouse
muffins
mugs
mushrooms
music

N

nail
narcissus
narwhal
NASA
nautilus shell
navel
neck
necklace
nectarine
needle
Nelly
Neptune
nest
net
newspaper
newt
New York
New Zealand
nightcap
nightingale
nine o'clock
Norman
nose
nurse
nut
nutcracker
nymph

O

oak
oasis
obelisk
oboe
ocean
octagon
octopus
office
okapi
Oliver
omelette
one
onion
oranges
orangutan
orchard
orchestra
osprey
otter
oval
oven
owl
ox

P

page
pages
pail
paintbox
paintbrush
painting
palace
pampas grass

panda
pantaloons
panther
papaya
papers
parcel
parrots
pasta
pastry
patch
path
pattern
paws
peacock
pear
peas
pedal
pelican
pencils
penguin
pepper
pepperoni (on pizza)
perch
piano
pie
pigeon
pillow
pin
pineapple
pink
pirate
pizza
plate
playing
plum
polar bear
pomegranate
pond
pool
postcard

pudding
pumpkin
Punch (as in "Punch and Judy")
puppet
purple

Q

quads (quadruplets)
quail
quarterdeck
quarters
quavers
Queen
question mark
quetzal (bird)
queue (waiting line)
quiche
quilted jacket
quince
quiver
quoits (rings)

R

rabbit
race
radio

radish
railing
railway
rain
rainbow
raindrops
raining
rake
ram
raspberries
rat
raven
reclining
red
Red Cross
red nose
reeds
reindeer
relaxing
ribbon
ring
ripples
river
road
Robin Hood
Robin Redbreast
rocks
rope
rose
round
rowboat
ruby
Rudolph
running

S

sail
salad
salami
sand
sandals
sand castle
sandwich
sapphire
sardine
sauce
saucepan
sausage
saxophone
scabbard
scarf
scarlet
scrub brush
sea
seagull
sea horses
seam
sea urchins
seed packet (for snowdrops)
seven (the Seven Dwarfs)
shadow
shamrock
shark
sheep
shells
ship
shirt
shoes
shreds
shuttlecock
skates
skirt
sky
sleeping (snake)

sleeves
slippers
smile
snail
snake
sneakers
snorkel
snow
snowdrops
snowflakes
snowman (*made of sand*)
soapsuds
socks
soup
soup bowls
spade
spaghetti
spider
spinach (*soup*)
sponge
spoons
spots
squirrel
stamp
starfish
stern
strawberries
stripes
submarine
submerged
sun
sunflower
sunglasses
sword

T

table
tadpoles
tail
tambourine
tangerine
tank
tapir
tarantula
tassel
teacup
teapot
teddy
teeth
telephone
tennis ball
tennis racquet
terrapins
thermometer
thistles
thorns
tiara
tickling
tiger
tiger moth
toad
toadstools
toast
toes
Tom Thumb
tomato
tongue
toothbrush
toucan
towing
toys
train track
treasure
treasure chest
triangle
trousers

trumpet
trunk
tulips
turban
turkey
turquoise (*colors*)
two

U

U-bend
udder
ukelele
umber-colored soil
umbrella
unbuttoned
uncork
undercurrent
underground
underhand
underneath
underpin
underwater
underwater lake
underwear
unicorn
unicycle
Union Jack (*flag*)
unique
United States (*flag*)
untidy
uproot
upside down
urchin
urn
U-shaped

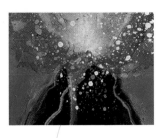

V

valley
van
vane
vanilla ice cream
vase
vegetables
vehicle
venetian blind
Venice
verandah
vermicelli
vest
viaduct
Viking
village
vine
violets
violin
viper
vol-au-vent (*on plate*)
volcano
vole
vultures

W

wagon

walking boots
walking stick
walkman
wall
wallaby
wallpaper
walnut
walrus
waltzing *(fish)*
wand
warthog
washing
washing line
wasps
watch
water
watermelon
waves
wavy hair
weather vane
wedding cake
    (looking wobbly)
Wee Willie Winkie
whale
wheels
whistle
white
wigwam
Wild West
willow
wind
window
wire
witch
woman
wombat *(with
    witch)*
wood
woodchuck
wood grain
wood louse

woolly hat
world
worm
wrist

X
X mark *(on ballot
    papers)*
X mark *(in tic-tac-toe
    game)*
Xmas lights
Xmas present *(with
    "X" sign for kiss)*
Xmas tree
X-ray fish
xylophone

Y
yacht
yak
yam
Yankee Doodle
yard
yarn
yawn
year
yellow
yeti *(footprints)*

yogurt
yolk
yo-yo
yucca

Z
zabaglione *(in bowl)*
zebra
zeppelin
zero
zodiac
zoo
zigzag
zip
zucchini